Morningtown Ride

words and music by
Malvina Reynolds

illustrations by
Michael Leeman

Turn the Page Press

Roseville, California

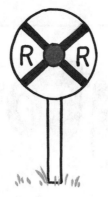

Words and music by Malvina Reynolds.
Printed at the Cal Central Press, Sacramento, California.

ISBN: 0-931793-00-9

for

Meghan

Special thanks to Carrie,
Bev and the Bos Family
Singers for their constant
encouragement.

Train whistle blowing, makes a sleepy noise,

Underneath their blankets go all the girls and boys,

Heading from the station, out along the bay,

All bound for Morningtown, many miles away.

Sarah's at the engine,

Tony rings the bell,

John swings the lantern to show that all is well,

Rocking, rolling, riding out along the bay,

All bound for Morningtown, many miles away.

Maybe it is raining where our train will ride,

But all the little travelers are snug and warm inside.

Somewhere there is sunshine, somewhere there is day,

Somewhere there is Morningtown,

many miles away.

Morningtown Ride

words and music by
Malvina Reynolds

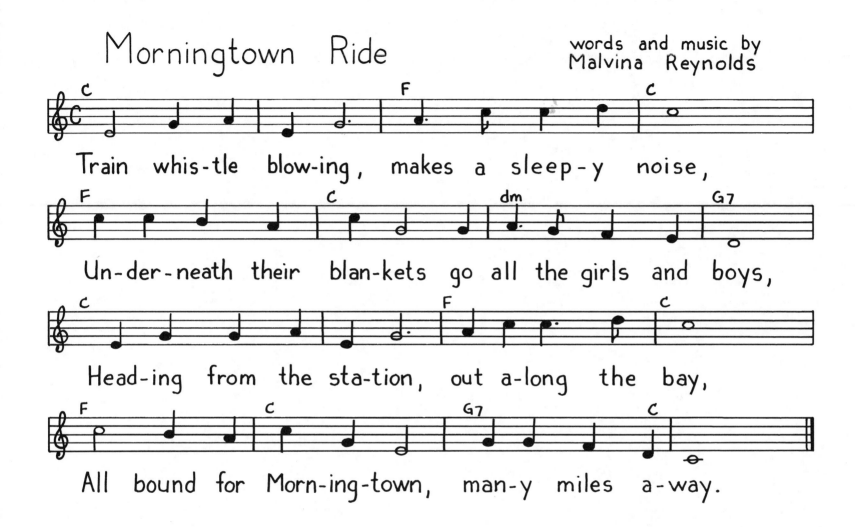

Train whis-tle blow-ing, makes a sleep-y noise,

Un-der-neath their blan-kets go all the girls and boys,

Head-ing from the sta-tion, out a-long the bay,

All bound for Morn-ing-town, man-y miles a-way.

Sarah's at the engine, Tony rings the bell,
John swings the lantern to show that all is well.
Rocking, rolling, riding, out along the bay,
All bound for Morningtown, many miles away.

Maybe it is raining where our train will ride,
But all the little travelers are snug and warm
   inside,
Somewhere their is sunshine, somewhere
   there is day,
Somewhere there is Morningtown, many miles
   away.